Mrs. Greenbe
Messy Hanukkah

Linda Glaser Illustrated by Nancy Cote

Albert Whitman & Company
Chicago, Illinois

The Story of Hanukkah*

A long, long time ago in the land of Israel, the most special place for the Jewish people was the Temple (synagogue) in Jerusalem. The Temple contained many beautiful objects, including a tall, golden menorah. Unlike menorahs of today, this one had seven (rather than nine) branches. Instead of being lit by candles or light bulbs, this menorah burned oil. Every evening, oil would be poured into the cups that sat on top of the menorah. The Temple would be filled with shimmering light.

At the time of the Hanukkah story, a mean king named Antiochus ruled over the land of Israel. "I don't like these Jewish people," declared Antiochus. "They are so different from me. I don't celebrate Shabbat or read from the Torah, so why should they?" Antiochus made many new, cruel rules. "No more celebrating Shabbat! No more going to the Temple, and no more Torah!" shouted Antiochus. He told his guards to go into the Temple and make a mess. They brought mud, stones, and garbage into the Temple. They broke furniture and knocked things down; they smashed the jars of oil that were used to light the menorah.

Antiochus and his soldiers made the Jews feel sad and angry. A Jewish man named Judah Maccabee said, "We must stop Antiochus! We must think of ways to make him leave the land of Israel." At first, Judah's followers, called the Maccabees, were afraid. "Judah," they said, "Antiochus has so many soldiers. His soldiers carry such big weapons and he uses huge elephants to fight his battles! How can we Jews, who don't have weapons, fight against him?" Judah said, "If we think very hard and plan very carefully, we will be able to defeat him." It took a long time, but at last the Maccabees chased Antiochus and his men out of Israel.

As soon as Antiochus and his soldiers were gone, the Jewish people ran to Jerusalem to clean their Temple. What a mess! The beautiful menorah was gone, and the floor was covered with trash, broken furniture, and pieces from the shattered jars of oil. The Maccabees built a new menorah. At first they worried that they would not be able to light their new menorah, but they searched and searched, until at last they found one tiny jar of oil – enough to light the menorah for just one evening. The Maccabees knew that it would be at least eight days before they could get more oil, but they lit the menorah anyway. To their surprise, this little jar of oil burned for eight days. The Jewish people could not believe their good fortune. First, their small army had chased away Antiochus' large army, and now the tiny jar of oil had lasted for eight whole days!

The Jewish people prayed and thanked God for these miracles. Every year during Hanukkah, Jews light menorahs for eight days to remember the miracles that happened long ago.

* The transliterated word *Hanukkah* can be spelled in a number of different ways – including *Chanukah*, *Chanuka*, etc.

To Helen, who opens her home and her heart to countless friends,
and who opened the way for this book. Thank you.—**L.G.**

To Mike—your tireless energy, compassion, and love are a gift to all,
but a treasure to me.—**N.C.**

Library of Congress Cataloging-in-Publication data
is on file with the publisher.

First published in the United States of America in 2004 by Albert Whitman & Company
ISBN 978-0-8075-5300-8

Printed in China
10 9 8 7 6 5 WKT 26 25 24 23 22

For more information about Albert Whitman & Company,
visit our website at www.albertwhitman.com.

1122/B0913/A4

Potato Latkes (for 4 or 5 people)

6 medium-sized potatoes
1 egg
1 small onion
3 T. (44 mL) flour, matzo meal, or bread crumbs
1 tsp. (5 mL) salt
oil—enough to almost cover latkes in frying pan

Rachel helps–Scrub and peel potatoes. Grate potatoes and onion. Pour off extra liquid. Add egg, flour, and salt. Mix.
Mama helps–Drop potato mixture into hot oil with tablespoon. Fry both sides until golden brown. Drain on clean towel.
Rachel helps–Clean up the mess.
Mrs. Greenberg helps–Serve hot with applesauce or sour cream.
Enjoy with friends!

"*Please* can we make potato latkes today?" Rachel sat at the kitchen table swinging her legs. "And let's invite Mrs. Greenberg for dinner!"

"Enough with the latkes!" Mama threw her hands in the air. "I told you already, we'll make them next week when the relatives come. *That's* when we'll invite Mrs. Greenberg."

FRANKIE'S
DOG
FOOD
LIST

"But tonight won't even feel like the first night of Hanukkah." Rachel took the menorah from the cupboard and pushed the first two candles in. "No latkes. No company."

"We'll still light the candles." Mama kissed her on the nose. "It'll be Hanukkah. Don't worry. But right now, Papa and I have lots of errands. So please get your coat on."

Rachel set the menorah on the windowsill. It was such a cold, grey day out there, just the kind that begged to make the house all warm and good-smelling. That gave her an idea.

"Can I stay next door with Mrs. Greenberg?"

"All afternoon?" Mama shook her head.

"Please?" asked Rachel.

"She's not so used to little monkeys." Papa gave Rachel a playful poke.

"But it's almost Hanukkah. And she's all alone," Rachel pointed out. "She could use a little company."

"Hmm. I didn't think of that. Well, I suppose..." Mama looked at Papa. "If you won't be any trouble..."

"I'm never any trouble!" Rachel pulled on her coat and raced out the door, hair flying.

“Wait!” Mama called after her. “I’ll telephone—just to make sure.” But Rachel was already skipping down the path.

31

Mrs. Greenberg's house was all clean and sparkly like it was just *waiting* for company, while Rachel's house always looked like it was still in bed with its hair sticking up. And Mrs. Greenberg was always glad to see her.

"Come in! Don't be a stranger," said Mrs. Greenberg. "I told your dear mama of course you can stay. It's much too empty around here—especially for Hanukkah."

Rachel stepped inside. "That's just what I told her." She peeled off her coat. "Can we make latkes?"

"Oh my," said Mrs. Greenberg. "I haven't made latkes in years."

"But latkes make it feel like Hanukkah," Rachel explained.

"It's some messy job," said Mrs. Greenberg. "All that grating and frying."

"But Mama and Papa would be so surprised!" Rachel jumped in the air.

"Hmm. I didn't think of that. I *do* have plenty of potatoes."

"Wonderful!" Rachel exclaimed. She skipped into the kitchen where everything had its very own place and it all sparkled, even the floor.

Mrs. Greenberg handed her an apron and they both got right to work grating potatoes. Rachel tried to keep her gratings in a nice little hill like Mrs. Greenberg's. But somehow her little hill slid right off the table.

"Oops!" said Rachel.

"Oy!" said Mrs. Greenberg.

COOKING
OIL
10 lb
Potato

What a mushy mess! Rachel grabbed the mop. But the more she mopped, the worse it got.

"That's OK." Mrs. Greenberg took the mop. "I'll finish later. Don't you worry. After all, what's a little grated potato between friends?"

Next it was time for the egg. Rachel tried to crack it into the bowl just like Mama always did. But somehow it popped right out of her hands.

"Oops!" said Rachel.

"Oy!" said Mrs. Greenberg.

What a slippery mess! Rachel grabbed the mop. But the more she mopped, the worse it got.

"That's fine. I'll finish later." Mrs. Greenberg stepped over the shiny yellow streaks. "Don't you worry. After all, what's a little egg between friends?"

She gave a sigh.

“Soon we’ll have Hanukkah latkes!” Rachel reminded her.

Mrs. Greenberg stirred everything in a big bowl.

Rachel lugged over a bag of flour. “Don’t we need this?” But somehow, the bag ripped. “Oops!” said Rachel.

“Oy!” said Mrs. Greenberg.

What a powdery mess! Rachel grabbed the mop. But the more she mopped, the worse it got.

"Never mind. I'll get it later," said Mrs. Greenberg. "Don't you worry. After all, what's a little flour between friends?" But she looked awfully tired.

“Soon it’ll feel like Hanukkah!” Rachel reminded her. And she sure hoped it would!

At last, it was time to fry the latkes. Mrs. Greenberg checked the clock. “Your Mama and Papa will be here any minute. Quick, Rachel, drizzle a little oil into the pan.”

“Mama uses *lots* of oil,” said Rachel. “For the miracle of when the oil lasted eight days.” But somehow, the oil came spurting out faster than Rachel had expected—much faster. “Oops!”

What a soppy mess! Rachel reached for the mop.

“Don’t even bother.” Mrs Greenberg sank into a chair in the living room.

COOKING
OIL

"Just let me rest a few minutes. Anyway, what's a little oil after all this?" She flung her arm at the kitchen.

Rachel waited for the part about friends. But not a word. And nothing about "Don't you worry" either. Uh-oh! The kitchen was such a mess—like it might faint if it looked at itself in the mirror. What would Mama and Papa say?

Just then, the back door opened. "Anybody home?" called Papa.

Mama stepped into the kitchen. “Oh no!”

“Surprise!” squeaked Rachel, trying to smile. “We’re making latkes.”

Mama and Papa did look surprised, but not the way Rachel had hoped. Not at all.

Papa pointed at the floor. "What's all this?!"

Mama frowned. "Rachel, look what you've *done.*"

Rachel's chin trembled. "I wanted to make it feel like Hanukkah. But I made a terrible mess." A tear slid down her nose. "I'm sorry."

OOKING

Mrs. Greenberg hurried over.

"Oh, *katchkeleh*, you dear little duck!" She rubbed the tear away with her thumb. "Actually, it's not a terrible mess. It's a *wonderful* mess. My house hasn't felt this lived-in in years."

"Really?" Rachel brightened up. "Well! I can make it lived-in anytime you want!"

Mrs. Greenberg laughed out loud. "Oh, darling, I'm sure you can!"

Rachel grabbed the mop. "Now let's *really* clean up!"
"I'll do it later," said Mrs. Greenberg.
"Don't be silly," said Papa. "Sit down and relax."
"That's right," said Rachel. "*We* want to do it."

Mama tied on an apron and fried up the latkes crispy and hot, while Rachel and Papa cleaned up. Now the house was all sparkly, warm, and good-smelling.

Mrs. Greenberg lit the candles and said the blessings.

Finally everything was just how Rachel had imagined. "Thank you, Mrs. Greenberg." She beamed.

"Don't thank *me.* Thank *you.*" Mrs. Greenberg grandly set the latkes on the table. "*I've* got latkes *and* company."

"You sure do!" Rachel hugged Mrs. Greenberg around her nice soft middle and gave a happy sigh. "Now *this* feels like Hanukkah!"